D1325903

This book belongs to:

. . . .

. . . .

Retold by Monica Hughes
Illustrated by Daniel Howarth

Reading consultants: Betty Root and Monica Hughes

Marks and Spencer p.l.c.
PO Box 3339
Chester, CH99 9QS

shop online
www.marksandspencer.com

ISBN 978-1-84461-571-1
Printed in China

The Three
Billy Goats
Gruff

MARKS &
SPENCER

Helping your child to read

First Readers are closely linked to the National Curriculum. Their vocabulary has been carefully selected from the word lists recommended by the National Literacy Strategy.

Read the story

Read the story
to your child
a few times.

But the bad troll jumped out.
"I'm going to eat you!" he said.
"No, you can't eat me!" said the
middle-sized billy goat.
"I'm just a middle-sized goat.
Wait for the big goat and eat hi

So the bad troll did just that.

Follow your finger

Run your finger under
the text as you read.
Your child will soon begin to
follow the words with you.

Look at the pictures
Talk about the pictures. They will
help your child to understand the story.

"I'm going to eat you!"

19

Have a go
Let your child
have a go at
reading the large
type on each
right-hand page.
It repeats a line
from the story.

Join in
When your child is ready,
encourage them to join in with the
main story text. Shared reading is
the first step to reading alone.

Once upon a time there were three goats.
They were the Billy Goats Gruff.
There was a little billy goat with
little horns.
There was a middle-sized billy goat with
middle-sized horns.
And there was a big billy goat with
very big horns.

There were three goats.

The three billy goats lived in a field.
They ate grass all day long.
There was a river in the field.
There was a bridge over the river.
There was a bad troll under the bridge.

There was a bad troll.

One day the little billy goat looked
at the field over the bridge.
The grass looked long and juicy.
He wanted to eat that grass.

So the little billy goat went onto
the bridge with a trip trap,
trip trap.

The little billy goat went onto
the bridge.

But the bad troll jumped out.
"I'm going to eat you!" he said.
"No, you can't eat me!" said the little billy goat.
"I'm just a little goat.
Wait for the middle-sized goat and eat him."

So the bad troll did just that.

"I'm going to eat you!"

Then the middle-sized billy goat
looked at the field over the bridge.
The grass looked long and juicy.
He wanted to eat that grass.

So the middle-sized billy goat went
onto the bridge with a clip clop,
clip clop.

The middle-sized billy goat
went onto the bridge.

But the bad troll jumped out.
"I'm going to eat you!" he said.
"No, you can't eat me!" said the
middle-sized billy goat.
"I'm just a middle-sized goat.
Wait for the big goat and eat him."

So the bad troll did just that.

"I'm going to eat you!"

Then the big billy goat looked at the
field over the bridge.
The grass looked long and juicy.
He wanted to eat that grass.

So the big billy goat went onto the
bridge with a thump, thump,
thump, thump.

The big billy goat went
onto the bridge.

But the bad troll jumped out.
"I'm going to eat you!" he said.

"I'm going to eat you!"

"No, you can't eat me," said the big billy goat.

"I'm a big goat and I have very big horns.

I will toss you into the air with my big horns."

So the big billy goat did just that.

"No, you can't eat me!" said
the big billy goat.

He put his head down and ran
at the bad troll.
He tossed the bad troll high up into
the air.
Then the bad troll fell into the river.
And that was the end of him!

The bad troll fell into the river.

Look back in your book.
Can you read these words?

goat

troll

bridge

grass

river

horns

Can you answer these questions?

Who lived under
the bridge?

What did the goats
like to eat?

What did the troll say to
the little billy goat?

First Readers

Read Together

Look out for other books in the **First Readers** range (subject to availability):

Fairytale Readers